# Angelina's™
## Lucky Penny

Published by Pleasant Company Publications
© 2003 Helen Craig Limited and Katharine Holabird
Based on the text by Katharine Holabird and the illustrations by Helen Craig
From the script by James Mason

Visit our Web site at **www.americangirl.com** and
Angelina's very own site at **www.angelinaballerina.com**

Printed in the United States of America

03 04 05 06 07 08 09 10 NGS 10 9 8 7 6 5 4 3 2 1

Angelina™
Ballerina

# Angelina's™
## Lucky Penny

PLEASANT
COMPANY
PUBLICATIONS™

"The Swan Princess! The Swan Princess!" Angelina and her best friend, Alice, sang together as they skipped down the path to ballet class.

"The best movie ever! And this afternoon, *we* get to see it," Angelina exclaimed. She couldn't believe their good luck.

Angelina skipped on, but Alice called to her, "Angelina, wait! Where's your ribbon?"

Angelina checked her head. "I had it on when we left home," she said. She searched the ground all around, but there was no sign of the ribbon. She would have to go to ballet class without it.

"Now you, Angelina," said Miss Lilly. Her students were practicing their steps for the big audition the next day.

Angelina leaped into the air, twirled around in a circle, and landed. But, oops! She wobbled a bit on her toes as she finished.

"Darling!" said Miss Lilly. "Think about those steps. You must be absolutely still after you've landed."

Angelina's face fell. She had tried so hard to keep still, but it was difficult. Would she ever get it right?

Angelina watched unhappily as Priscilla Pinkpaws took her turn and landed perfectly.

"Beautiful, darling!" chimed Miss Lilly. "You see, Angelina, that is how you must do it!"

Angelina tried to push away all her bad feelings. She would just have to work harder, she decided.

"Come on, Angelina, or we'll be late for the movie," said Alice after class.

"I'm sorry," Angelina said firmly, "but I can't go to the movie. I've got to go home and practice my dance routine."

Alice walked Angelina part of the way home. They played leapfrog along the path. As Angelina sprang over Alice's shoulders, she felt her bag slip off her arm. The bag slid along the ground and stopped just short of a puddle.

When Angelina bent down to pick up the bag, she noticed a coin lying in the puddle.

"Hey, it's a lucky penny! It stopped your bag from getting wet," said Alice excitedly.

And then Angelina spotted something else. "You're right, it *is* a lucky penny. Look what I found!" she said, lifting her hair ribbon from the tall grass beside the path. She tied the ribbon on her head and said, "Hurry up, Alice! We're going to be late for the movie, and we still have to get Henry."

"But, Angelina, don't you need to go home and practice?" asked Alice.

Angelina shook her head. "I've got a lucky penny. I don't need to practice!" she said as she raced off down the path.

Angelina, Alice, and Henry searched for three empty seats in the village hall. As they sat down, Henry turned to Angelina and whispered, "Please, can I see it now, Angelina?"

Angelina handed the lucky penny to her little cousin. "Be careful, Henry. It's very special," she said. She turned the coin over and showed him the date. "See? That's the year I was born!"

"Oh!" gasped Henry.

When the lights dimmed, Angelina hastily dropped the penny back into her bag. She was so excited about the movie that she didn't notice that the penny missed the bag. It bounced on the floor and rolled away into the darkness.

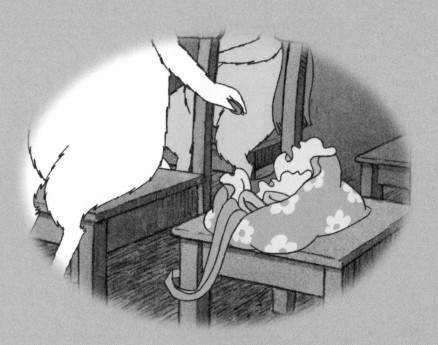

"Priscilla Pinkpaws will be so disappointed when I get the part," said Angelina as the mouselings walked home after the movie. "Watch this!" She sprang along the path, spun around in the air, and toppled suddenly to the ground.

"Wha-what happened?" Angelina stammered. "Where's the penny?"

"I'm sure it's in your bag," said Alice. But it was *not*. Angelina dumped her things onto the ground, and Alice and Henry helped her sort through them. The penny wasn't there.

Angelina's heart sank. "It's gone," she sighed. "No wonder I can't do the steps. We've *got* to find that penny!"

The mouselings rushed back to the village hall. The doors were locked, but Angelina saw that two wooden planks in the back door were loose. She pushed the planks apart and tried to squeeze through the gap, but she was too big.

"Will you try, Henry?" she pleaded with her cousin, who was the only one small enough to fit.

Henry peered through the gap. He didn't like the dark, but he wanted to be brave for Angelina. "Al-alright," he squeaked as he squeezed his little body through the crack.

"Just look for anything round and shiny," Angelina called after him.

A moment later, Henry popped back out. He proudly
dumped an assortment of shiny round objects on the
ground.

"Well done, Henry!" Angelina praised him as she and Alice
began sifting through the objects. But there was no penny.

"I'm sorry," Henry said in a tiny voice as he walked home beside Angelina.

"It's not your fault, Henry," said Angelina. She took Henry's paw and gave it a squeeze.

"Shouldn't you be at home practicing, Angelina?" a voice called from down the street. Priscilla and her twin sister, Penelope, were sitting on a low stone wall.

Angelina tried to ignore them, but Henry said boldly, "She doesn't need to practice, 'cause she found a lucky penny!"

The twins fell into a fit of laughter. "A lucky penny!" howled Penelope. "There's no such thing."

Priscilla jumped off the wall and began to twirl. "Besides," she said, "I don't need luck. I'm the best dancer!"

Angelina knew that Priscilla *was* a good dancer. And now that the lucky penny was gone, Angelina would have to work very hard to earn the part.

Angelina practiced her ballet steps late into the evening. Again and again, she leaped across her room, spun into the air, and landed in front of her mirror.

"I've nearly got it!" Angelina said aloud after landing firmly on her toes. But she returned to her starting position and practiced the steps again. They had to be perfect!

When Angelina and Alice arrived at Miss Lilly's Ballet School the next morning, Henry was waiting for them. "This is for you, Angelina!" he said proudly, holding out his paw. "It's your lucky penny."

Angelina grasped the penny and checked the date. "Well, Henry, you clever thing!" she exclaimed.

Priscilla watched them from across the room. She made a face at Angelina, but Angelina just smiled back at her.

"Take your places, darlings!" called Miss Lilly.

Priscilla's audition was first, and she performed the steps perfectly. When she was finished, she stepped back into line, very pleased with herself.

"And now, Angelina, it's your turn," announced Miss Lilly.

Angelina took a deep breath and stepped forward. She let the music carry her across the dance floor. She leaped gracefully into the air, twirled around, and landed steadily on one slipper, her eyes closed and her arms stretched upward.

As Angelina waited nervously, Miss Lilly and a lady from the Theater Royal spoke together in hushed voices. They reviewed Miss Lilly's notes and then smiled at each other. Miss Lilly nodded her head.

"Now, my darlings," she said dramatically, "the results. Angelina will dance the part!"

The mouselings gathered at Henry's house after the
auditions. Angelina spun Henry around and hugged
him tightly.

"Oh, Henry!" she exclaimed. "Thanks to you, I got the
part! But where on earth did you find my penny?"

Henry untangled himself from Angelina's arms and reached under the bed. He pulled out a glass jar full of pennies. "I've got lots of lucky pennies!" he announced.

Angelina and Alice looked at each other with wide eyes, and then giggled. Angelina knelt beside Henry and held out the penny he had given her. "Will you look after this for me, Henry?" she asked.

"Okay!" said Henry brightly. He dropped the penny into his jar and said, "I'm going to be very lucky, aren't I?"

"You *are*, Henry," Angelina said tenderly. "You are."